© Editorial Playor
Adapted and published
in the United States by
Silver Burdett Company
Morristown, New Jersey

1985 Printing

ISBN 0-382-06807-6 (Lib. Bdg.)
ISBN 0-382-06949-8

Library of Congress
Catalog Card Number 84-50431

Depósito legal: M. 33.201-1985
Edime, S. A. - Móstoles (Madrid)
Printed in Spain

Silver Burdett Company

CLASSICS FOR KIDS

MOBY DICK

Herman Melville

Adapted for young readers by Joanne Fink

illustrated by Hieronimus Fromm

Call me Ishmael. I have always liked adventures. None seem as daring as hunting whales. The whale is the largest and most powerful animal on earth.

In my time they were chased in swift sailing ships and caught with harpoons. Harpoons are like strong lances. The people who throw harpoons are called harpooners.

I went to New Bedford hoping to find a whaling ship that I could sail on. In an inn there I met Queequeg. He was a huge harpooner. His father was the king of the island of Rokovoko.

In spite of his fearsome appearance Queequeg was very good-natured. We became friends. The two of us went to Nantucket to find work on a ship.

It wasn't easy to get a job on a whaling ship. There was one, though, that needed men. It was called the *Pequod*, but sailors were afraid to talk about it.

Queequeg and I decided not to pay attention to any rumors, so we signed on. We soon found that there were many strange things being said about its owner, the mysterious Captain Ahab.

On the ship Queequeg and I met two other harpooners. One was an Indian called Tashtego and the other an African named Daggoo. That night the first mate, Mr. Starbuck, gave the order to set sail in search of whales.

After a few days of sailing, I heard the lookout shouting with excitement. They were the words we had all been waiting to hear—"There she blows! There she blows!" We were already near a group of those huge animals.

Captain Ahab brought us all together and told us a terrible story. Once an enormous white whale had sunk one of his ships and eaten his leg. This whale was known as Moby Dick. It was the largest white whale in the world.

Ever since then Captain Ahab had sworn to chase Moby Dick to the ends of the earth. He wanted revenge. After the way he described his fight with this monster, it was easy to imagine what Moby Dick looked like.

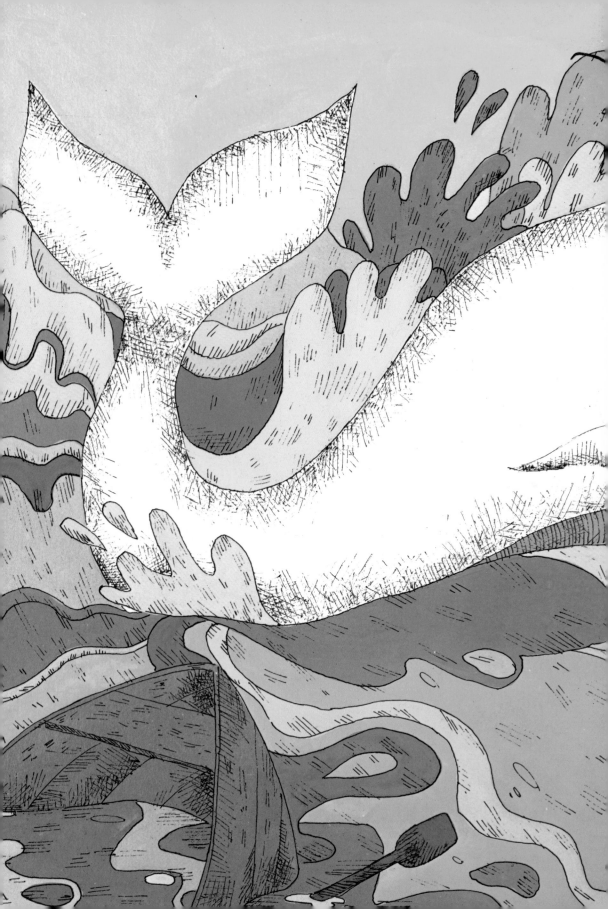

Captain Ahab hated Moby Dick. He hated the huge whale so much that he had an Oriental fortune teller on the ship. His name was Fedallah, and he was supposed to lead us to the spot in the huge ocean where the white whale was hiding.

The sailors were superstitious. They thought that Fedallah would bring bad luck to the ship and all the crew.

One day we lowered a whaling boat into the water. We were going to chase a whale. It was a large whale but not as large as Moby Dick. Suddenly the animal charged us. With one sweep of its tail, it upset our tiny boat. We all had to swim back to the *Pequod*.

After days of searching we suddenly heard Ahab shout, "A giant whale off the starboard side! It's Moby Dick!" For three days we hunted down Moby Dick in our whaling boats.

On the first day of the chase, the mighty whale got a tooth caught on a whale boat. He turned the boat over, throwing Captain Ahab and the crew into the sea. On the second day the whale swam toward the boats. This time he charged right into Ahab's boat. Once again everyone was thrown into the sea.

On the third day we set out once more in the whaling boats. Again we sighted Ahab's mortal enemy. There were dozens of harpoons already stuck in this cunning whale's back. As we neared the whale, Captain Ahab threw his harpoon. When it stuck in the whale, it seemed to make the creature angry.

With great fury Moby Dick turned toward the *Pequod*. It was as if the whale wanted to wreck the ship!

I closed my eyes so that I wouldn't have to see the awful crash. The force of the blow was so strong it threw me into the air. The *Pequod* broke in two and quickly sank.

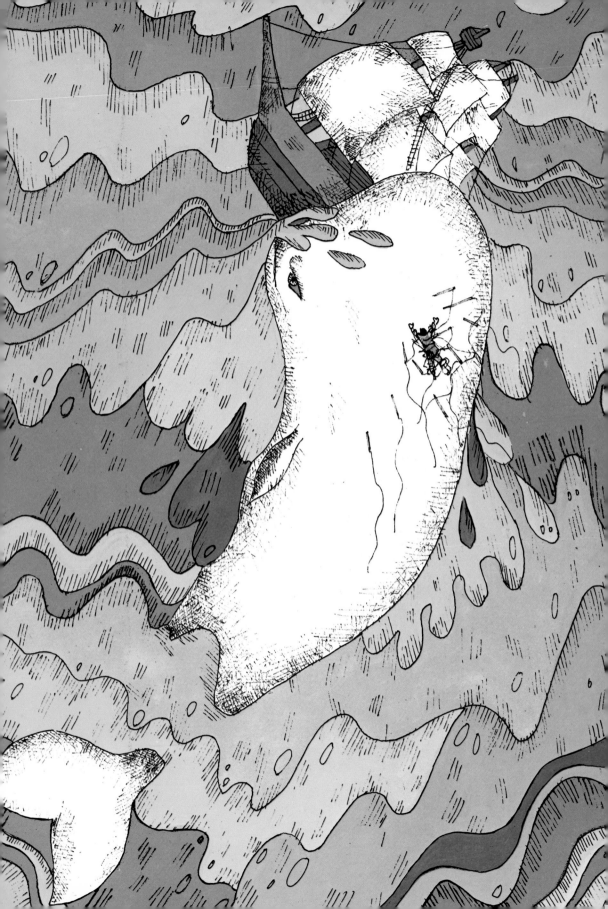

Captain Ahab's whaling boat was still afloat. When he saw what the whale had done to his ship, he went into a rage. Quickly he threw another harpoon into the huge whale. The rope from the harpoon became wrapped around Ahab's neck. As the whale swam away, he pulled Ahab up out of the boat and into the sea. The captain was caught and killed by the very monster he had hunted for so many years!

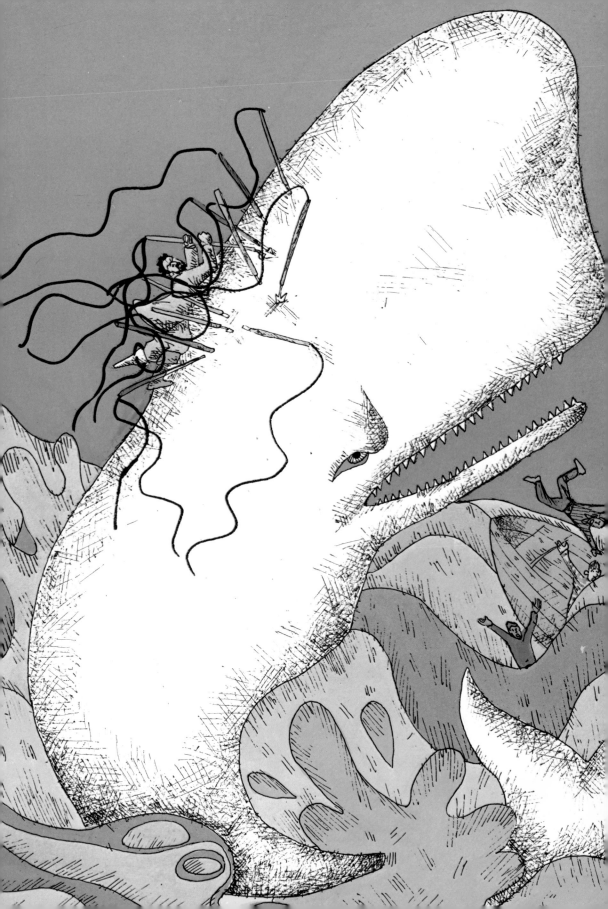

I hung on to some of the wreckage from the ship. For two days I drifted in the ocean. Then I was rescued by the *Rachel*, another whaling ship.

Everyone else from the *Pequod* was lost. I was the only one to survive and tell the tale of the strange passion that had cost Captain Ahab his life.